P9-EDK-741

Anna Grossnickle Hines

BETHANY FOR REAL

GREENWILLOW BOOKS
New York

FOR THE REAL BETHANY
WHO REALLY CAN BE
ANYTHING SHE WANTS TO BE

First Edition 10 9 8 7 6 5 4 3 2 1

Library of Congress Cataloging in Publication Data

Hines, Anna Grossnickle.
Bethany for real.

Summary: Bethany makes a new friend while
trading pretend lemonade for a pretend kitten.
[1. Play—Fiction] I. Title.
PZ7.H572Be 1985 [E] 84-5927
ISBN 0-688-04008-X
ISBN 0-688-04009-8 (lib. bdg.)

Bethany pulled her wagon down the street.
Cloppety-clop, cloppety-clop went her feet.
She neighed loudly.

She clopped up to Laura's lemonade stand.
"Look at me, Laura," she said. "I'm a horse."
But Laura wasn't there. Just some cups and an empty pitcher.
Bethany poured herself a cup of pretend lemonade.
"Umm!" she said. "Very good lemonade today."

Someone was listening. Bethany turned around. A boy was looking at her. He was holding a big cardboard box.

"This is my place," she said.

"I know," he said. "I'm just visiting. My grandma lives over there."

"Oh," said Bethany. "Would you like some lemonade?"
"Yes, please."
Bethany poured from the empty pitcher and handed him the cup.
"Where's the lemonade?" he asked.

"It's pretend," Bethany said.

The boy pretended to drink it.

"What do you have in that box?" she asked.

"Kittens," the boy said. "Brand-new ones."
Bethany looked. The box was empty.
"They're pretend," he said.
"Oh," said Bethany. "Could I hold one?"
"Okay. Just be very careful and don't take the black one. It's my special one."

Bethany picked up a make-believe kitten and gently stroked its head. "I like kittens," she said. "I wish I had one to keep. Daddy says they make me sneeze, so I can't have one really, but I could have one of THESE kittens."

"THESE kittens are mine," the boy said.

"I'll trade you some lemonade for one."
"Okay. Two cups of lemonade for one kitten," he said.
Bethany poured the pretend lemonade and handed him two cups.

"I like this gray one," she said, taking a make-believe kitten from the box. "I'll name him Moonpie."

"This one is Cola," the boy said.

Bethany watched him pet his pretend kitten.
"I'm Laura," she said.
"I'm Timothy Andrew Miller, but you could just say Timmy if you want."
"Okay, Timmy," said Bethany. "Let's take our kittens for a ride."

Timmy held the kittens and Bethany pulled the wagon. A big girl was walking toward them on the sidewalk.

"Hi, Bethany," the girl said.

It was the real Laura.

"We're playing," Bethany said. "We're taking our kittens for a ride."

"What kittens?" said Laura. "I don't see any kittens."

"Right here. This one is Moonpie and that one is Cola. Moonpie is mine. Timmy gave it to me."

"You don't have any kittens," Laura said.
"That's just dumb."
"It is not dumb."
"It is so."
"Is not!"
"Is so! It's very, very dumb!"

“Well, anyway, I’m not Bethany!” Bethany said.
“She’s Laura,” said Timmy.

"She is not! She's Bethany! I'm Laura!"
"You are not!" shouted Timmy.
"I am, too! I ought to know who I am!" said Laura.
"Well, you aren't Laura!" Timmy shouted.

"Yes, she is," said Bethany.

"She is what?"

"She IS Laura."

"No, you're Laura," Timmy said.

"No, I'm Bethany for real and Moonpie isn't even my kitten. Really, Moonpie is yours, Laura."

"Mine?" Laura said.

"Yes," said Bethany. "I traded your lemonade for him."

"But there wasn't any lemonade left," Laura said.
"For pretend there was," said Bethany.
Laura looked at her. "You traded MY pretend lemonade for this pretend kitten?"
"Right," Bethany said, "so it's yours."
"Oh," said Laura. She reached out to Bethany's hand and took the make-believe kitten.

Bethany and Timmy watched as she held the handful of air to her cheek.
"He's purring," she said.
Bethany nodded. "He always does that."

Laura held Moonpie carefully. "You can be Laura if you want," she said. "I'll be Bethany today."

Bethany smiled.

"And you can keep Moonpie. I'll get another kitten."

“I still have some in the box,” Timmy said.